I Love  My Pirate Papa

I Love My Pirate Papa

Laura Leuck

Illustrated by Kyle M. Stone

SCHOLASTIC INC.
New York Toronto London Auckland
Sydney Mexico City New Delhi Hong Kong

I love my pirate papa!
He's the bravest buccaneer.
He helps me put my earring on
and buckles up my gear.

At dawn we hoist the anchor,
raise our flag up in the breeze,
so Jolly Roger's face will warn
the sailors on the seas.

I get to walk along the plank
and leap into his lap.

I've learned the letter X
because he lets me read his map.

He shows me how to climb the stays.
We shimmy up the mast.

And when we spot the distant shore
I get to yell, "AVAST!"

"LAND HO!"

we yell to all our mates
as we head toward the land.

And then I help him haul the chest
we dug up in the sand.

When we're finally back on deck
he divvies up the loot,
then tosses me a bag of coins
I hide inside my boot.

He takes me to the galley
where we taunt our tired crew.
We bang on Cooky's kettle
if he's snoring near his stew.

Dinner's grub and grape juice,
we're sure to chomp and slurp.
Then we have a contest:
Who can belch the biggest... BURP!

And when the sun slips from the sky
he tucks me in my bunk.

He reads a book on Captain Hook
I keep inside my trunk.

Then Papa kisses me good night
and dims the lantern's glow.
He whispers softly in my ear
before he turns to go:

"I spent my life a-plundering.
My treasures bring me joy.

But there's nothing I prize
more than you,

my dearest pirate boy."

ISBN 978-0-545-26809-7

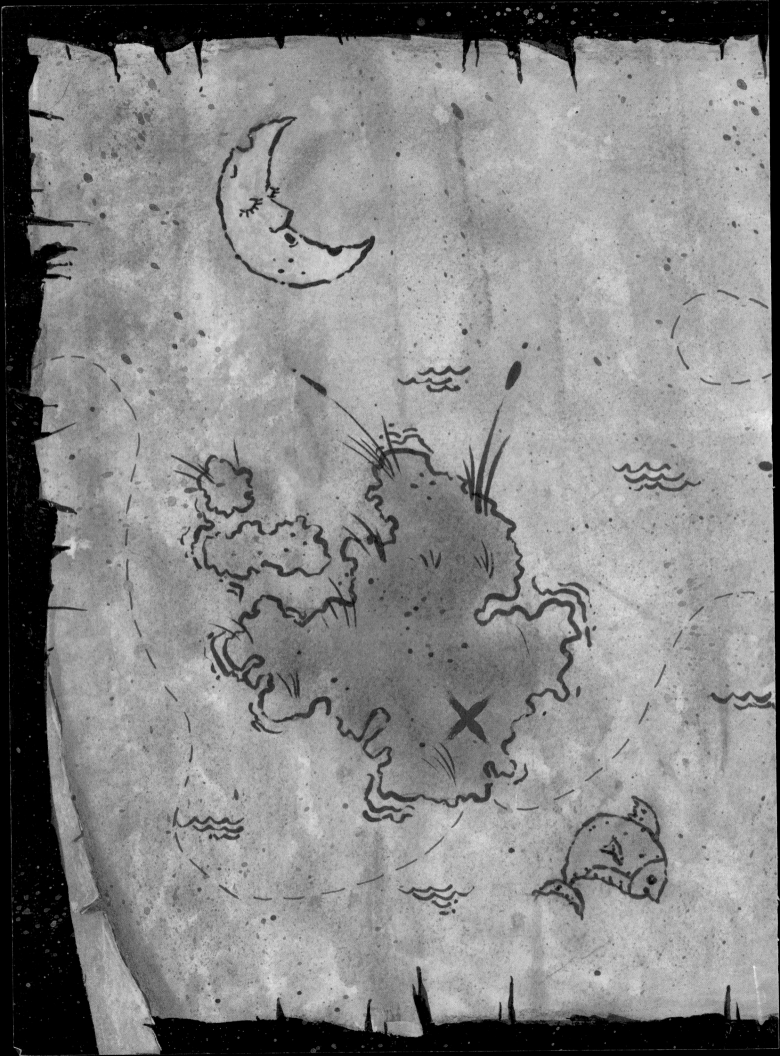